Man
of the
MATCH

Man of the MATCH

SOPHIE SMILEY

Illustrated by
MICHAEL FOREMAN

Andersen Press • London

First published in 2005 by
Andersen Press Limited,
20 Vauxhall Bridge Road, London SW1V 2SA
www.andersenpress.co.uk

British Library Cataloguing in Publication Data
available
978 1 84270 420 2

Phototypeset by Intype Libra Ltd
Printed in the UK by CPI Bookmarque, Croydon, CR0 4TD

Reprinted 2006, 2007 (twice), 2009

*Author's royalties to Camphill Village Trust
(Botton Village)*

To Timothy and Benita Smiley,
and Victor and Greta Brooks

Chapter 1

'Camping?' Bobby banged my bunk with both feet.

'Not today!'

'Tents?'

'No. Go back to sleep.'

Every morning, for a whole week, he woke me. He was all jittery, like a goalie waiting for a free kick. We were waiting to go to Special Camp – a holiday for children with special needs and their siblings. That's me. Bobby's sister. His sibling. Bobby loved that word. When he first heard it, he ran round the room yelling, 'Sib-ling, sib-ling,' like a fire engine.

At last the big day arrived. Bobby woke me at three o'clock. And four o'clock. And five o'clock. By six o'clock he was all dressed up in his beloved goalie top, and raring to go!

We set off for Bobby's school. It's different from mine because he's got Down's syndrome. I used to get jealous, as he goes in a taxi. Once, I even asked, 'Mum, why can't I go to a special school?'

She said, 'You're special just as

you are. We need a girl on our team.' You see, my mum and dad are so football mad that they wanted enough children for a football team. They ended up with a five-a-side: Wembley, Semi, Striker, Bobby and me! My daft dad gave us all football names. Bobby and I are called after his World Cup hero, Bobby Charlton. Some people think Charlton's a funny first name, but I think it's lucky; perhaps I'll be the first girl to play in a World Cup final!

Well, that Saturday, the whole team was there to wave us off. Wembley swung Bobby round by his ankles, Semi twirled a football rattle, and Striker dribbled a ball

in and out of the bags, did a
nutmeg round the driver and
scored a goal through the coach!

Looking around the
playground, I recognised nearly
everyone. Most of the helpers
had been on the holiday play
scheme. Laura, a pretty girl from

Bobby's class, was clinging to her mother. Her brother, Sean, hissed, 'Baby,' then pinched her when he thought no one was looking. I was glad he wasn't my brother.

There was just one boy, by himself, who didn't go to Bobby's school. It was a hot day, but he was wearing a coat with fur round the hood. His head was bowed, as if he didn't want to look at anyone. Bobby noticed him too, and went over.

''Ello,' he said.

There was no response. Bobby put his head on one side, leant close and said, ''Ello,' again. He looked around, and asked, 'Sibling?' He expected everyone on the camp to have a sister, like he had.

A grey-haired woman stepped forward. 'This is Paul. I'm his care worker. He doesn't talk. Perhaps you'll keep an eye on him for me?'

Bobby put an arm around

Paul's shoulder and said, 'Friends?'

But Paul shuffled away from the hug, and stared at his trainers.

'C'mon, Paul.' Bobby beckoned him onto the coach. Paul followed at a distance, flicking his hood strings. As we pulled out of the playground, Wembley, Semi and Striker ran along trying to keep up with us, Mum shouted, 'Don't forget to write,' and Dad sang, 'Here we go, here we go, here we go!'

The care worker made for her car, and Paul pulled his hood right down over his nose.

Straight away Bobby began unpacking his lunch box.

'San'wich, Paul? Crisps? . . .
Biscuit? . . .'

Paul just flicked his hood
toggles faster and faster, while
Bobby ate the whole packed
lunch before we'd even left town!
Every time one of the staff

walked down the coach, Bobby's
face lit up and he asked,
'Football? Beat the goalie?' and
they answered vaguely, 'We're
going to do lots of great things.
Games. Music. Drama.'

I had this funny feeling that
their ideas about what to do at
camp, and Bobby's, might not be
quite the same.

You see, Bobby had set his
heart on spending the whole
camp doing nothing but football.
And I think he'd already decided
to make Paul his man of the
match.

Chapter 2

Dear Mum and Dad,

It was difficult to write, all squashed up in my little tent, but I knew Mum would be leaping out and doing terrifying tackles on the postman until he brought her a letter from us.

The food is funny, the helpers are cool, and there are spiders in my

*tent! When we arrived Bobby
danced onto the campsite, with his
kitbag on his head, and his arms
flapping up and down! Expect you
can guess what he did next. Yup!*

You're right. Go straight to the top of the Premier League! He built a goal post. Well, his first one was made of tent poles. But then Tom (d'you remember the helper from play scheme – with the wacky hair?) made him hang a tent over them, and put his sleeping bag in. So next, he got hold of two lanterns. There was this terrible sound of glass breaking – Paul had hit the 'post'. Then, just before supper, they were taking shots at the back of an old truck when the farmer's dog leapt out. Bobby jumped into Tom's arms, and didn't let go of his hand till bedtime!

Last night I had a nightmare about Bobby building goal posts everywhere, and they started coming to get me! When I woke up, I went to wake Paul and Bobby, but their tent was empty. Paul's pyjamas were folded all neatly, but – surprise, surprise – Bobby's stuff was spread across the field. Just like home. I picked up his teddy and towel and stuff – they were in a trail leading to the river. You'll know how I felt as I got nearer, and heard the water. There were these two posts, right at the edge, and I had this picture of Bobby shouting, 'Save!' and diving over the bank. I got all panicky, and started calling his name. Then Tom came along and told me that Paul and Bobby were helping Chris with the breakfast. The 'goal' was just two rotten old fence posts – doh! Rushing over to the kitchen I found Bobby

*serving. He was holding this bottle
of food colouring, dishing out dollops
of porridge (bright RED porridge),
and singing, 'Come on, you reds!'*

*After breakfast there were music
and games, but not football. Bobby
wasn't pleased. He had that 'I'm
planning something' look on his
face. I was keeping an eye on him
until Sean came over and said, 'Bet
you can't climb that tree.' He went
first – boasting about how great he
was – and got stuck! Tom had to
rescue him – ha ha. Then Fizza and
I went up. We got so high the camp
looked titchy. I spotted these two
trees miles and miles away, with
someone in between them. I was sure
it was Bobby in his latest goal.
Fizza said I needed glasses – it was*

only a scarecrow! Then I saw something red floating down the river, and I nearly fell out of the tree. I thought it was Bobby in his goalie top. Fizza laughed and said it was just an oil drum. She thinks I'm nutty – she says she doesn't see her brother, Ali, popping up all over the place.

I stopped shaking when we got to the top. It was brilliant. All the matchstick people waved at us. Fizza teased me on the way down – she kept pointing to a sheep, or a bird and shouting, 'Look, it's Bobby!' and 'There's a football stadium!' Then, just when she'd convinced me not to see another phantom goal post ever, I heard Bobby shout, 'Shoot, Paul, shoot.'

You'll never guess where his new
goal was. Right in front of the
serving table. Well, Paul kicked.
Bobby dived. The ball hit a table leg
and the pot of stew wobbled over the
edge.

Bobby wasn't a bit bothered. He
just lay in the grass, with the dinner

22

trickling past his nose, waggling his
fingers in the gravy and licking
them. Chris caught the pot and
yelled, 'Save!' while Janet said,
'Don't get in a stew, Chris!' and
then Tom started singing:
   'Walk on, walk on, with hope in
      your heart,

23

And STEW'll never walk alone!'

Since then, Bobby's been dribbling a ball round the field, singing, 'Stew'll never walk alone' at the top of his voice. He made us all sing it at campfire.

Write and tell me the midweek score, and how Semi's team got on. Lots of love,

Charlie

PS   Q: What do you call a nervous camper?

A: TENTS!

PPS   Q: What do you call a serious camper?

A: In TENTS!

PPPS Q: What do you give an unhappy camper?

A: AtTENTion!

Chapter 3

After I'd put my letter in the
camp postbox, I said goodnight
to Bobby. He was half in and half
out of his sleeping bag, like a
Jack-in-the-box, while Paul was
tucked right in, with the
drawstring pulled tight round his
face. I didn't mind sleeping on
my own. I'm not afraid of the
dark. Not afraid of anything, me
– well, perhaps just one thing.

But anyway, I liked the sound of the wind rustling in the trees, and the canvas flapping, and I was soon fast asleep.

Early in the morning I had a dream of a spider dancing up and down my arm. It danced quicker and quicker. And the tune it was dancing to was somehow familiar. It reminded me of . . .

'Bobby?' I called out.

Sure enough, Bobby's hand had slid under the tent door and his fingers were pattering in panic on my arm!

'Charlie,' a small voice whimpered from outside. I struggled to unzip the tent. He was shivering and his lower lip was beginning to wobble.

'Moo,' a cow bellowed.

Bobby leapt into my tent and dived down the sleeping bag.

'Moooo,' went the cow, even louder, and Bobby's head disappeared. I started humming:

'When you walk through a storm,

Hold your head up high.'

Gradually Bobby stopped shaking, and I could feel him relax to our football anthem:

'And don't be afraid of the dark.'

'Cows!' Bobby corrected.

So I sang it again, 'And don't be afraid of the cows.'

Bobby began to join in. I came to the last bit and sang:

'Walk on, walk on with hope in your heart,

And you'll never walk alone.'

Bobby giggled and sang out his own final line:

'Moooo'll ne-ver walk a-lone!'

Even the cows joined in his chorus!

Five minutes later he was sound asleep.

Chapter 4

When the gong clanged, I had to shake Bobby awake. And he was still sleepy after breakfast as we all sat round. Only Paul wasn't part of the big circle: he hovered a little way away, not looking at anyone. Dave, one of the adults, stood up. He was big and bearded, and wore a ballet tutu over his jeans! Bobby hid his head in embarrassment, while

Dave twirled, waved a magic wand, and announced: 'Today we're going to do painting and weaving.'

'Beat the goalie?' Bobby asked.

'Perhaps later.'

Bobby's face fell. I held my breath, waiting for what might happen. But he only muttered grumpily, and followed me to the craft area.

'Look, Bobby.' I cut a potato in half. 'You can print footballs on your bag.'

Blob, blob, blob he went, making a wall of heads. Blob, blob, blob went the potato, in a Beckham banana kick. Pow! And Bobby was off to the painting.

Paul worked more slowly. He

covered every centimetre of his bag with neat lines, each circle placed carefully, one above the other.

Laura couldn't manage printing, but she laughed as Tom helped her swoosh a paintbrush. Her brother watched. Leaving his printing, he walked past casually, kicking a pot of water over her paper as he went by. I glared at him, and he said, 'Accident,' all innocent. I was about to stick a leg out to trip him, when Bobby stepped in.

''Ere you are, Laura,' he said, holding out a new piece of paper. 'Paint it red.'

Then he went to have a go at weaving. Janet held out two sticks and Bobby wound wool around them. It was fiddly work, and he soon left it and wandered off, with Paul following like a silent shadow. I could hear him singing, 'Three lions on my shirt' as I printed a bag for Mum. She always says, 'Everything's fine if Bobby is singing. It's when he stops you have to watch out.'

As I pressed the last potato, the singing stopped. There was a noisy silence spreading from beyond the tents, the kind of quiet that deafens a stadium before a penalty.

I scrambled up, to find out where it was coming from. Hurrying past the kitchen fire, and up the hill, I reached Bobby's tent. He was so absorbed in his work that he didn't notice me approach. I stood and watched his fingers flying in and out. Paul walked behind him carrying balls of wool – oranges and yellows, and some sparkling with gold thread. Bobby wove the wool between the tent and a tree, up to a washing line, and down to the tent pegs. It was the strangest, most wonderful goal post I'd ever seen!

Finally, he turned to Paul, and said proudly, 'I's a golden goal, Paul!'

And I thought I saw Paul's hood move, just a little, as he darted a look at Bobby's creation.

'Shoot, Paul, shoot,' Bobby urged.

With his head down, and his
fingers flicking, Paul kicked the
ball to the left. Bobby threw
himself – whoomph – flat out,
hands and feet flying through the
air, through the goal, and into the

tent! The canvas collapsed
around him, and Bobby
disappeared.

Paul stood on the spot, rocking
anxiously from foot to foot while
the tent staggered. It lurched, and

fell forward. Then it tumbled down the hill – a twirling, golden meteor, coming to a halt in a circle of surprised people. It chuckled. A set of fingers emerged – fluttering, waggly fingers, playing their own special music.

Then out popped Bobby's head. He grinned and asked, 'Football, anyone?'

Paul loped across the grass. Perhaps I was imagining things, but I thought I noticed a slight nod come from inside his tightly tied hood.

Chapter 5

'We're off to see the farm today,'
Chris announced next morning.

Bobby shook his head fiercely.

'You'll like it,' Janet said, 'there
might be some lambs.'

'Football,' Bobby said.

'Not now. Everyone's going to
the farm.'

The rest of the camp gathered
by the footpath.

Bobby sat down and I knew

that a battle was about to begin.

Tom came over to see what was wrong. 'Come on,' he called, 'there'll be a treasure hunt.'

Bobby buried his head in his crossed legs.

'Football!' he said.

'You can kick a football along the path,' Tom tried. 'Perhaps the farmer's got a dog who takes penalties.'

Bobby didn't move.

'Penalties here!' He wasn't budging.

What would Mum do? Grabbing a plastic plate, I flashed it in front of him, and said, 'Red card!' in my firmest voice.

There was a muffled, 'Not goin',' and I knew it was useless.

He was a striker on strike.

'Come on, Charlie – leave him,' said Fizza. Everyone else was moving off. I was desperate to follow, but it's hard when you're a team.

'You go on,' said Tom, 'I'll stay with him.'

I turned to go, but my feet wouldn't move. I was going to miss the treasure hunt, the animals, the special tea.

'It's not fair,' I said crossly.

The grown-ups huddled round Bobby, an anxious team round an injured player. Wordless. Not knowing what to try next.

Then Paul moved. He'd been standing so quietly that I hadn't even noticed him. Like a good striker, he always had his own pool of space. Now he edged towards Bobby. Surprised, everyone else moved back. Paul crept forwards, taking tiny steps. He hovered above Bobby, rocking. Bobby didn't move, but I could tell he knew Paul was there. The toggles of Paul's coat swung, gently ruffling Bobby's hair. Two eyes peeped out. The toggles moved faster. Bobby's fingers pattered. Then, like a swimmer bursting for air, Paul started running off across the grass. Startled, Bobby looked round, scrambled to his feet, and followed. Sometimes, a player works some magic on a pitch, and you just blink and think,

'How did he do that?' Well, we all stood, staring after the disappearing figures, blinking!

Paul and Bobby arrived at the farm passing a ball between them. They were greeted by the farmer's wife who gave everyone baskets, and sent us off on an egg hunt. For a few minutes Bobby forgot about playing football and dashed about between the barn and the yard, searching through piles of hay.

'Look over here,' I called.

When he saw the speckled,
brown hen's egg his face
crumpled.

He shook his head, saying,
'Not real!'

'Yes it is.' I passed it to him.
He licked it gingerly, and then,
before I could stop him, he took

a big bite! Golden goo exploded everywhere, and Bobby spat in disgust.

'Not chocolate!' He looked at me accusingly.

And it was only then I realised that Bobby thought we were hunting for Easter eggs!

Wiping his mouth, he sloped off to get some target practice against a wall. I could hear the ball thud as I sat eating a cream tea in the farmer's garden. The strawberry jam was thick and gloopy on the crumbly scones. I soaked up the sun and the scene and the . . . SILENCE! I remembered Mum's words.

Where was Bobby?

Suddenly, Paul tore past and

clambered frantically onto a tractor.

There was a scream!

I stood up and gaped in horror at Bobby's latest goal. He had opened the five-bar gate. And there he was, frozen, in the middle of his open gate-goal. And standing in front of him was the ugliest, hairiest striker I'd ever seen! It lowered its head to the

ground, hunched its huge
shoulders and snorted. Flying
forwards, it hurtled towards
Bobby. Then, with a quick flick of
its horns, it tossed the ball up,
past Bobby, and into his goal.

Bobby didn't even see the ball.
His eyes were glued to the bull. It
banged a hoof in applause, then
trotted off to join a crowd of
spectating cows.

Bobby walked backwards in a wobbly way, picked up his precious football, then sprinted up behind Paul on the tractor. The red-faced farmer dashed across and clanged the gate shut. Paul pushed back his hood, and turned the steering wheel round and round, while Bobby swung the gear stick. A wobbly wail floated from the tractor:

'Hold your head up high, and don't be afraid of the cows.'

Everyone in the farmyard started joining in:

'Walk on, walk on, with hope in your heart, and you'll never walk alone . . .'

The colour flooded back into Bobby's face, and his voice

swelled across the farmyard in his favourite refrain:

'Moooooooo'll neeeeeeeeever walk aloooooone!'

Chapter 6

I'm pretty brave about most things: spiders; heights; bullies. I can usually take care of anything. But there was one place at camp I'd avoided all week – until the last afternoon.

I was busy carving a totem pole with Fizza when Chris announced, 'Watersports at the river!'

The river! My heart pounded

as I remembered the day Kevin Joggs pushed me into the deep end of the swimming pool. I have these nightmares where I struggle to breathe and thrash about, desperate to get out. Then I wake, and Mum's there, all the blankets on the floor, and me gasping for air.

'Watersports!' Chris repeated.

For the first time since we'd left home I wanted Mum. Really wanted her, so badly I could feel a knot in my stomach. I'll go to my tent – pretend to be poorly, I thought.

I was just about to slink away, when Janet walked up. 'You've got some post,' she grinned. The envelope was covered in Dad's cartoon drawings of our favourite players. Still trembling at the thought of the water, I ripped it open.

Dear Charlie,

Thanks for your letter. Glad you're both conTENT at camp.

It was my inTENTion to clear the shed while you were away, but I found a set of Bobby's football annuals in there, and I'm reading them instead! I'm planning – TENTatively – to paint your room. Mum will show me the red card if I don't!

We won 2–0 on Tuesday – great save by Will Brooks –

and Semi's team drew 3–3,
equalising in the ninetieth
minute.

  Love, Dad

PS Q: *What does an octopus*
      defender do in a game
      of camp football?
  A: *A TENT-tackle!*

Oh Dad! He can always make me
laugh, and suddenly I missed him
so much. He would know how
scared I was.

But getting his card made me
see something else. Dad would
never pretend to be ill to get out
of something. He'd never run
away. It would be like those
players who fake injury to get a
penalty. We don't have any time

for them in our house. I fought back tears, feeling sick at the very thought of the water, but not wanting to let Dad down.

Then there was a slight fluttering on my arm. A light pattering. No words, just the rhythm of gently drumming fingers.

'Bobby!'

There are some things Bobby understands better than anyone else. So when he tugged my hand, I followed him down to the bank.

Two logs spanned the river. In the first game, people had to walk across a plank, carrying a mug of water, and empty it in a bucket on the other side. Chris asked for volunteers, and the two teams lined up. I sloped off to sit with the spectators. Bobby was jigging up and down, eager to start, but his team didn't have enough players.

'We need one more person,' Chris called out.

I knew I couldn't do it, not over all that water.

'C'mon, Charlie,' Fizza called.

I shook my head.

'Scaredy cat, scaredy cat!' Sean shouted.

That did it! My knees wobbled as I stood up. And I thought, this is how it must feel in a World Cup penalty shoot out. You step up, and the whole world is watching you, and your heart's

banging out an anthem of terror!

'Be all right,' Bobby patted my
arm.

And the next moment, the race
started! Tom and Jacob, wearing
silly dresses, flippers and
snorkels, set off! They trotted

across easily. Bobby went next for
our team. He walked backwards
across the log, arms flapping, and
the water in his mug wobbling.
Reaching the far side, he skipped
off the log and took a bow!
Everyone cheered. We were well

ahead when Max began. He went too fast, and almost at once – splash – he was in the water. He paddled back to the bank and started again. This time he crept across with tiny tiptoe steps, and two of the other team overtook him. Then it was Chonka's turn. He sat on the log, and pulled himself forward on his bottom, holding the mug between his teeth. Across from him Nadia fell in three times, and we began to draw level – until there were just two people left: Sean and me.

The water was murky. I could hear Dad's voice saying, 'Hold your head up high!'

A much louder voice in MY head said, 'Sharks!'

But I made myself step onto the log.

'Swim low, sweet Charlie 'ot,' Bobby sang from the opposite bank.

I kept my eyes glued to Bobby's face; he willed me on. I was half way across when a huge spray of water soaked me. Sean had fallen in. I'd be next. I froze. Couldn't go on. Couldn't go back. The water in my mug trembled. I started shaking. Any second now and . . .

'Splosh!' There were thrashing sounds. My knees were giving way.

''S all right, Charlie, 's all right.'

There, below me in the water, rushing to my rescue, was Bobby.

57

'One step, Charlie, tha's right.'

My foot inched forward.

'One step, two step, tickly under there,' Bobby sang as he swam along beside me. 'Big step, Charlie!'

I didn't look across at Sean, but I could sense it was a photo finish. We were level. It felt like the eighty-ninth minute of a match. I had to score. I flung myself forward onto the mud, and a great cheer went up. Bobby scrambled up the bank, shook water over everyone, then jumped onto me, all arms and legs, and together we twirled around the field singing, 'We are the champions!'

Chapter 7

Bobby looked at the buckets
where everyone had emptied
their mugs. The two FULL
buckets of water. Glancing
around like a pantomime villain,
he picked up a bucket, crept up
behind Tom, and threw the water
over him! Tom grabbed the other
bucket and soaked Bobby; soon
everyone was joining in a massive
water fight. It only stopped when

Chris called out: 'What do you call the thing that carries electricity?'

'A pylon?' said Tom.

'That's right – PILE ON!' and everyone piled on top of Tom!

The afternoon continued with water slides, water pistols and raft building. Bobby joined in each activity, but every few minutes his voice piped up like a referee's whistle, 'Football?'

And one of the helpers would say, 'Not now. It's watersports today.'

Bobby scowled.

There was a lull before tea. 'Sleeping lions!' someone shouted, and we all lay in a line with our heads on each other's tummies. The first person giggled, and a rippling roar of laughter zigzagged down the chain. I listened for Bobby's chuckle. Strange. I glanced around at all the bouncing heads and bellies. No Bobby. I scanned the field for his mop of red hair, for Paul's hunched, hooded figure. It was empty! I got up and hurried across the grass, through the cowpats and nettles, and back to the water. The river coiled like a snake. The water was dark and murky where we'd stirred it up. I strained to see through the darkness.

I looked around wildly. There, in the distance, walking beside the willows, was a figure, on its own. It looked familiar, but strange: a boy in jeans and a tee shirt. Then I realised. It was Paul. Paul, WITHOUT his coat! But where was Bobby?

'Paul,' I called, trying to keep the panic from my voice. 'Where's . . .'

Tom emerged from behind Paul. He seemed to be watching the water. What was he staring at?

Seconds later, Bobby floated round the corner and sailed into sight. He was standing astride a raft, dressed in his swimming trunks and goalie top, waving a football rattle.

Tom, hovering in the background, gave me a thumbs-up sign. And I realised he'd been

with them all the time, watching.

And I realised, too, that Mum
was right when she said, 'You
don't have to look after him,
Charlie.'

By now, everyone had gathered
to watch Bobby's triumphal
entry. A kingfisher shot in front of

him, a turquoise striker zipping
through the defence. Bobby
threw a football at Paul and
announced: 'It's water football
time!'

Paul kicked from the bank, and
Bobby flung himself – whoomph
– flat out, grabbing the ball

before crashing into the water.
He emerged, draped in reeds and
weeds and water lilies, spurting a
great fountain from his mouth
and chanting, 'Whaddasave,
whaddasave!' He leapt and
stretched, soared and dived until
the dinner gong went. And that
afternoon, Bobby kept a clean,
but very wet, sheet!

Chapter 8

'Mooo . . .' The cows woke me early on the last morning. I waited for a frightened Bobby to leap into my tent. Instead, I heard him bellowing, 'Moo off, cows!'

After a farewell hokey cokey, we trudged up the hill towards the coach. Bobby darted round the cowpats, pretending he was dodging defenders in a run on goal. As he rounded the brow of the hill, Tom and Jacob leapt out, wearing top hats and waving magic wands. A row of children and adults were lined up like a wall of defenders; they were hiding something.

Tom waved his tent pole wand, and chanted:

'Abracca dabracca, Abracca dole,

Turn this tent pole into a . . . GOAL!'

Everyone moved aside to reveal a magical, end-of-camp goal post! The uprights were made from the farmer's crooks. Ballet tutus, potato print flags and flippers dangled from the crossbar! The staff started singing, 'There was

Bobby, Bobby, mad about his hobby, in the stores,' as Tom said, 'For our last trick we have our very own Beat the Goalie competition!'

Jacob snipped a pink ribbon and declared the goal officially open. We all lined up for our shots, and Bobby flew across that goal front like Superman! He saved every shot.

Paul lined up last. 'Shoot, Paul, shoot!' Bobby shouted.

All week Paul had run up with his head turned away from the goal. He always shot to the left. We held our breath, waiting for the last approach. Bobby jigged on the spot. Paul ran up. He swung, and kicked. Bobby dived

left. The ball powered to the right, and into the back of the goal.

Everyone gasped. Bobby blinked, and rubbed his eyes. Then he slumped into a heap, burying his head in his lap. My heart sank. Bobby was going to refuse to budge, and no one would be able to get home. We'd be stuck at camp for ever and ever.

Paul rocked from foot to foot, not looking at Bobby, but inching closer. I thought I heard a soft humming of a familiar tune. I couldn't work out where it was coming from. But Bobby instantly looked up. His eyes widened. Then he walked up to

Paul. Holding out his potato print bag, he announced: 'Man o' the match, Paul!' A tiny smile played on Paul's mouth.

All too soon it was time to leave. The sun shone, but Paul had his coat back on. He pulled the hood down and flicked his zip, faster and faster. He didn't like the coach, and I suddenly realised how he felt: all trapped like a player being man-marked. He shot little glances around, a striker searching out a space.

'Awright, Paul?' Bobby sensed the unhappiness too. I could tell by the look on his face that he was trying to think of something to cheer Paul up. Looking for a distraction he said: ''S my birthday soon, Paul.'

Paul twiddled his coat toggles.

'July the thirtieth.'

'The day England won the World Cup,' I said proudly.

A soft voice added: '1966, Wembley, England 4, Germany 2.'

The voice came from somewhere deep inside a hood!

''S right. Wembley!' Bobby whooped.

I wanted to whoop, too: Paul was talking!

The whole coach fell silent.

'What about 1994?' Tom said.

'1994, USA,' the soft voice from the coat continued, 'Brazil 3, Italy 2. Penalties.'

'34?' Jacob asked.

'June 10th, Italy. Italy 2,
Czechoslovakia 1,' Paul chanted.

Dates and times poured out in
a rich river of words.

Bobby's eyes shone as he
watched and listened.

All too soon we drew up in the
school playground. Paul rushed

for the coach door, rocking from foot to foot as he waited to be let out. Bobby tried to follow, but people blocked the gangway. He stood on his seat and yelled, ''Bye, Paul, 'bye!'

As the doors hissed open I watched a coat hood, trimmed with fur, nodding.

Then, very softly, from deep inside, I heard the words, 'Wembley, 1966, Bobby, Charlton,' and after a short pause, 'Friends!'

And Bobby and I chorused back, 'FRIENDS!'

About the Author

Sophie Smiley was born in a Dominican monastery – she says she had a very happy childhood surrounded by Fra Angelicos and Ethiopian priests! She now teaches English and is also a staff member of Forest School Camps, working with both the able and those with learning difficulties. She is married and has two children and they all live in Cambridge.

About the Illustrator

Michael Foreman is one of the most talented and popular creators of children's books today. He has won the Kate Greenaway Medal for illustration twice and his highly acclaimed books are published all over the world. He is married, has three sons and divides his time between St Ives in Cornwall and London.

Have you read the other
books about Bobby, Charlton,
and their football-mad family?

Bobby, Charlton and the Mountain

Bobby wants a football kit for the
Queen's visit to his school! Money-
making muddles, a beastly bully, and a
breathtaking penalty shoot-out lead to a
VERY unexpected meeting . . . !

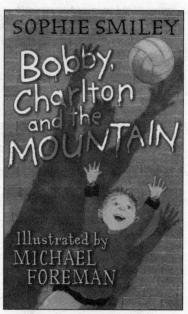

ISBN 9781842701782 £4.99

Team Trouble

Bobby and Charlie are terribly concerned when big-brother Semi gets ill. He becomes incredibly grumpy, and will only grunt at people – and worst of all, he doesn't seem to like football any more. Whatever can be wrong with him? Will the girl he meets mysteriously help bring him back into the family team?

ISBN 9781842706848 £4.99

Pirates Ahoy!

Charlie's football-mad family
have moved their pitch to the beach,
and her brother's on a quest for a
pirate adventure. It's all hands on deck
as footballs become cannonballs and
damsels in distress are rescued. But
will Bobby ever find his hidden
treasure? And will Charlie even
win him back to football?

ISBN 9781842708828 £4.99